BLACK HOLE RADIO

ANN BIRDGENAW
ILLUSTRATIONS BY E.M. ROBERTS

DFP

DartFrog Plus

Published 2021

Printed in the United States of America

ISBN: 978-1-953910-48-6 (paperback)
ISBN: 978-1-953910-49-3 (ebook)

Library of Congress Control Number: 2021905406

Publisher Information:
DartFrog Books
4697 Main Street
Manchester Center, VT 05255

www.DartFrogBooks.com

*I dedicate this book to my family,
my favorite readers.*

CONTENTS

PROLOGUE

Do you believe in black holes, wormholes, wrinkles in time?

Do you ever think about space travel? Alien encounters? Amazing adventures?

If not, you should close this book now.

OK, so you're a believer. Then you just might be ready to hear what happened to me on the most intergalactic day of my life.

My best friend Matt and I have our own outer space club called '*Uranus is the Butt of the Solar System*' (UBSS). We're the only members so far, but with a catchy name like that, it's sure to be very popular.

My name is Hawk. I was named after Stephen Hawking, only the most famous cosmologist and astrophysicist EVER. So I think this was destined to happen to me since the day I was born.

CHAPTER 1

STAR TREKKERS

Everyone in my grade five class is super excited right now because it's Friday, 3:14 in the afternoon and we're all counting the seconds. One minute to go before the weekend starts! Mrs. Bupkiss tries to remind us about our math assignment, but no one is paying attention. Everyone is ready to run out the door. Matt is coming over for a sleepover in 'Mission Control' and we're going to watch a new episode of our favorite show, *Star Trekkers*.

The bell rings and we all crash out the door. I stumble out into the hallway looking for Matt, at the same time trying to avoid bumping into Big Mikey. That's something I don't need right now; a run in with the class bully. He's been after me all week to pay him some cookie money. I'm not going to do it. What would my Grandpa say? He'd tell me to stand up to this bully. But Grandpa's not around anymore and I still can't believe it. I get sad whenever I think about him. He died a month ago but I haven't really cried or anything. What is wrong with me? I just want to go home and sleep all weekend. My mom thinks I've been sleeping too much lately, so she arranged for Matt to come over tonight and get me back into my space club stuff.

"Hey, dude!" Matt yells as we link fingers, do an interlocked fist pump, and then click our rings together for our secret space club handshake. We both have a National Space Agency (NSA) club ring. It's guaranteed to be anti-alien with ultrasonic sound and reflectors. So cool! We ordered them from the back of my favorite magazine, *Spaced Out.*

"This is going to be great!" Matt says, grabbing his backpack and pulling his hoodie up over his wild afro. "I can't wait to see the Star Trekkers hitch a ride on Halley's Comet to wipe out the devilish dust bunnies of Nebula."

"Ya!" I reply, "The last episode was so epic when they rounded up the mad mutant Martians from Venus."

"Right! But why were they from Venus if they're Martians?" Matt asks me again.

Oh, brother. Matt is not the best at figuring out plot twists.

"Because they mutated, remember?" I say patiently.

"Oh, right. That was so...so... Out There!" he says pointing up to the sky.

The school bullies, like Big Mikey, call us super cosmo-nerds. But I prefer Astro-geniuses, thank you very much.

Guess I got that from my Grandpa, who was the original Astro-genius. He taught me many things, but the most important was that the more we explore outer space, the more we can appreciate Planet Earth. There are billions of planets, moons and stars in the universe, but none as special as our blue planet. Not to mention, no ice cream, no TV, no...

"C'mon Hawk!" Matt shouts, pulling me out of my

thoughts, "Let's blast off!" he continues, as we head for our clubhouse.

"OK, let's go, bud." Matt's good at cheering me up.

We're at ground zero, 'Mission Control'--actually it's my dad's old tool shed that's connected to our garage. It's totally cool inside with lots of posters of planets, an old computer, buttons and knobs on the wall, and glow-in-the-dark stars for a super-cool effect at night. And the 'piece de resistance' (that means the best part) is a real telescope for scanning the Milky Way for UFOs. It's my Grandpa's old telescope, he gave it to me when we started the club. He always said he had a special connection to the cosmos and that I was a chip off the old asteroid ... in other words, just like him. He had promised to share something important with me when I was old enough, but he never got the chance. I wish I knew what he wanted to tell me.

"C'mon, Hawk, let's get the TV out here! It's almost time to watch Star Trekkers!" Matt shrieks, helping me carry the TV from the garage.

I think he's had too much moon pie and rocket candies, but I'm glad he's here. I'm feeling better already. "OK, OK. Pass the rocket candies over here, Matt," I say taking a big slurp of my favorite drink, cola and milk.

"Uggg! How do you drink that stuff?" Matt asks covering his eyes like he can't even look at my brown and white soda.

We watch the Star Trekkers use a giant interstellar space vacuum to suck up the last of the devilish dust bunnies. "Um, Hawk, why is Nebula so dusty?" Matt asks, as he pops some cotton candy fluffs into his mouth, melting them like sugary dust bunnies.

Matt thinks I'm actually a genius like Stephen Hawking.

"Nebula is Latin for 'cloud of dust' because that's what it's made of and sometimes..." Just then, I'm interrupted by a beeping sound.

Beep, beep, beep, beep.

"Did you hear that?" I ask Matt.

"What?" he says.

Beep, beep, beep, beep. It sounds again!

"That," I answer, looking around our clubhouse.

Beep, beep, beep, beep.

"Hawk, I think it's coming from the garage," Matt says.

Beep, beep, beep, beep.

We both get up and walk towards the connecting door to the garage.

Beep, beep, beep, beep!

"It's getting louder, dude," Matt whispers.

"Why are you whispering?" I hiss.

"I don't know...it could be a burglar's watch or something," Matt replies.

Beep, Beep, Beep, Beep!

I pause. I hadn't thought of that. But the beeping is making me curious.

"Let's check it out. We're Star Trekkers, remember." I say, to give Matt some courage (and me too).

Beep, Beep, Beep, Beep!

"It's probably nothing," I say, opening the door to the garage.

Beep, Beep, Beep, Beep!!

"It's much louder in here, Hawk!"

"I know that. I can hear! But where is it coming from?" I exclaim.

"Over there." Matt says, pointing towards a box in the corner of the room that also seems to be glowing a bit.

"What the...."

CHAPTER 2

WHAT IS IT?

We climb over boxes, bikes, and tools to the corner where my dad keeps the old stuff that he got when Grandpa died last month. One of the boxes is beeping.

Beep, Beep, Beep, Beep!

"Open it!" Matt says.

"You open it," I say.

"No, you should! It's your garage," Matt insists.

I guess he has a point.

"OK, stand back," I say as I reach toward the box and open the top.

Beep, Beep, Beep, Beep!

A soft green light emanates from the bottom of the box.

Beep, Beep, Beep, Beep!

I clear out the box, pulling out a photo album and some old hiking boots, and look down into the depths. "What is that thing?" I ask Matt to look in.

"Whoa, looks like a small radio," he exclaims, "The alarm must be set."

Beep, Beep, Beep, Beep!

"Just turn off the alarm and everything will be right with the world again," Matt says, reaching for the small, square transistor radio. Click. He pushes the alarm switch to off, and we both breathe a sigh of relief.

Beep, Beep, Beep, Beep!

"What!?" we say together.

"I know what to do," I say, picking up the radio. "We have to take out the batteries."

I open the back and pull out the ancient-looking batteries. "There. That should do it, Matt. Let's go back to our show," I say, turning around to go back to the safety of our clubhouse.

Beep, Beep, Beep, Beep!

The glow is getting brighter, casting an eerie green neon light over everything.

"OK. This is getting creepy Hawk," says Matt "Let's go get your dad."

"Wait. I can fix this!" I say, shaking the radio and pulling out the antennae, "I just need to change the tuner like this and....."

We hear a sound like static coming from the radio — crackling and popping sounds like a bad connection getting louder and louder.

Covering my ears, I can hear Matt shouting, "Hawk. Let's get out of here!"

I feel the hair on the back of my neck standing on end and a shiver runs down my spine.

"This can't be good," I say as I sense a gravitational force drawing us toward the radio.

Matt and I try to back away in the other direction to the exit, but the pull is so strong we can't get away.

An old lamp in the corner tips over and slides along the floor towards us, its cord trailing behind like a slithering snake. The overhead light flickers and boxes start to shake and rattle like they're being pulled by a strong magnet.

"Heeellllpppp!" I shout, as I feel us getting sucked into the eye of the radio's electromagnetic force field.

The last thing I see is Matt's shocked, greenish face as I grab onto his arm.

We tumble head over feet in zero gravity through a tunnel that seems to stretch and shrink, tilt and straighten, while brilliant beams from cool flames flash by us at light speed, illuminating the darkness around us. Pop! And then there's nothingness.

CHAPTER 3

THIS ISN'T GOOD

"Ahhhhhh," we scream together as we are sucked through the spiraling tunnel and spit out the other end. Pop!

"Ahhhhh," still screaming, we bounce down a hill and do a face plant.

"Ptooey." Matt spits out sand "What just happened?" he asks, spitting again, getting to his feet.

"Not sure," I say, tilting my head and knocking red dirt out of my ears, "but we're not in my garage anymore."

I stagger to my feet and I can't believe my eyes. Where the heck are we? I think about calling for my Dad but realize he won't be able to hear me. We've been blasted to the Sahara desert or something. But how is that possible? The sky is a weird shade of yellow that I've never seen before and the air is hot and hard to breathe. I see nothing but red sand and rolling hills of more red sand. We do a 360 and there is still only red sand for miles around.

Matt looks at me and his eyes go wide. "What are those birds doing, Hawk?" he asks, pointing behind me. I turn to see what look like drones in a V-formation like Canada geese coming at us. My Grandpa bought me a drone for my tenth birthday and showed me how to use it. But these look like tiny attack helicopters from the *Attack of the Drones* movie!

"Run, Matt! Those aren't birds they're cosmic drones and I think they mean business." I stop worrying about where we might be in the Universe and start worrying about how to stay alive on this red planet.

We run in the opposite direction, but we hear a deafening whir as the flock of drones gets closer and we sense their sonic vibrations getting stronger.

We take a dirt dive to get away from them in the nick of time, as the drones buzz over our heads.

Matt lifts his head and yells, "Missed us, you flying chickens! Ptoo!" as he spits out sand.

"M-Matt, w-w-what are you trying to d-d-do? G-g-get us k-k-killed?" I sputter through a mouth full of sandy dust.

"What are they going to do to us? Shoot us down like a couple of .... Aaaaa!"

"Run!" I yell. Zzzt, Zzzt, Zzzt! Lasers hit the ground all around us, making red sand fly up in every direction, as we dodge the drones again. "Serpentine, Matt!" I scream over my shoulder.

"What?" Matt yells back, confused.

"Run serpentine, like this!" I shout running in a snake-like pattern. "Faster!"

"Quick question," Matt says catching up to me, panting. "Where are we and why are these flying chickens trying to kill us?" he gasps, running across my path.... "And what is wrong with your garage!?"

"That's three questions," I reply, jumping over a laser blast. "And we have bigger things to worry about right now, like staying alive!" I shout, crisscrossing in front of him. "...And I don't think we're on Planet Earth anymore. Run faster!"

As the drones get louder and closer, we can see their tiny laser guns pointed in our direction, as they get ready to come in for the kill. I turn around in desperation. I flash my club reflector ring at them as they bear down on us. The laser beam hits my ring and reflects back toward the first drone, but misses. He circles us and joins the end of the attack formation.

"Too bad you missed, now they know we have a weapon," pants Matt, as he runs across my path.

I notice a large crater up ahead and motion for Matt to run towards it. We dive in and turn around to see the drones flying low to get a good shot at us. I get ready with my ring and wait for the perfect moment to use it. The second drone waits till the last second to start shooting his lasers. I hold my hand up with the ring pointed right at the drone and keep my head low. One of the beams hits the reflector, which I have aimed right back at the drone, and the laser hits it head-on. The drone explodes with the pieces taking out all the other ones behind it, and they all fall like dominos. Only the first one avoids the flying shrapnel and flies off, probably to alert the leaders.

We jump up and look around at the carnage of smashed drone pieces everywhere. "That was cool!" says Matt, his eyes as big as saucers. That's when I notice that we aren't the only ones looking at the drone massacre. In the distance, we see what looks like some really, really, mad mutant Martians. *If they're Martians, are we on Venus?* My head starts to swim as I feel like we've been transplanted into our favorite TV show. But it's not as fun as I thought it would be.

CHAPTER 4

ENCOUNTERS OF A WEIRD KIND

"Call 9-1-1! Call the Star Trekkers! Call my mommy!" Matt cries, leaping back into the deep crater. Sheesh, if this is a dream, I hope we wake up soon. This is getting embarrassing.

"Pull yourself together, Matt," I say, jumping in after him, shaking him by the shoulders. "We have to think this through. What would the Star Trekkers do?"

We take a chance and peek over the top of the crater to see the tallest and ugliest alien gliding towards us. He has long spindly arms and fingers that look like grey tentacles. Big black eyes, in a grey, balloon-shaped head perched awkwardly on a long skinny neck that looks like it could never hold up such a monstrous skull....and, and where's his mouth? OK, so *we're definitely not on Planet Earth anymore.*

I look over at Matt because he's yelling, "They're coming, Hawk! What are we going to do? At least Star Trekkers have weapons."

"Quick, try your ring, it's supposed to be anti-alien. It worked for me," I say, looking around in desperation.

Matt sticks his hand out of the crater and wiggles it around.

"Greetings, aliens from another planet," we hear the leader say loud and clear and ...*Wait! What? He speaks English ...and who's calling who aliens!*

"Matt, did you hear that? They must have thought you were waving at them! They seem friendly...and speak....human."

"Show yourselves, heroes. We are a peaceful planet and mean you no harm," one of them says.

We look at each other and clamber out of the crater and walk nervously towards the tall one and his odd-looking group. OK, *if this is a dream, it would be a good time to wake up! Wake up now!*

Coming towards us are eight seriously strange-looking aliens. They all have grey balloon heads, huge black eyes but, no ears, nose or mouth. No, wait, their mouths are on their necks! Their long, dangly arms hang down at their sides and they are wearing long robes so their feet are not visible. But do they have feet? I see something peeking out from the bottom of their gowns! I try not to panic and I avert my eyes, afraid to see more. *Gulp!*

"Matt, they think we're heroes for some reason. Maybe they won't vaporize us after all. Follow my lead," I whisper out of the side of my mouth.

"Hey, where are we? We didn't mean to destroy all your drones, sir, errr mister alien-sir. We don't know how we got here and ....," I ramble nervously, trying to keep up with him as he glides away on long.... *tentacles? Is this really happening? Because if it is, it's getting weird!*

The aliens turn and motion for us to stay quiet and walk with them. We do as we're told; it's not every day that you meet for real aliens.

"Whoa, what's happening?" Matt cries and grabs

onto me. An incredible futuristic city appears out of nowhere. Things we had only seen in movies and on *Star Trekkers*. Colorful glass, mirrors and shiny metals create a cityscape we could never imagine. Monorails swirl around overhead, through buildings, schools and parks with odd-looking plants and trees, with blue and red leaves and multicolored flowers. Little aliens zip around on hover-boards. And they're all staring at us with their big oval-shaped eyes.

"The protective shield has lifted," says the leader. "We need it to protect our peaceful citizens from the bullies of planet Boogernaut."

Matt and I look at each other and cover our nervous giggle -- *Planet Boogernaut!*

"Yes, it was their drones you destroyed, and we are in your debt for saving us! You are both our heroes!"

"But we..." Matt starts to say and I shoot him a 'Let me do the talking' look.

"Please, can you help us get home to Planet Earth in return?" I ask him.

"That is not possible!" says the leader, shaking his balloon-ish grey head from side to side.

Matt and I look at each other as if we are about to cry. *Heroes aren't supposed to cry!*

CHAPTER 5

BE CAREFUL WHAT YOU THINK

"I'm...Hawk a-a-and this... is Matt," I stammer nervously to the tall one.

"I know," he says, "we use ESP to communicate here."

"ESP...you mean..."

"Yes, extra sensory perception. We read each other's thoughts. We know you are very far from your home planet, Earthlings," says the leader.

Oh, man! I remember my first impression of the leader...tall...ugly...

"Err, doesn't that cause a lot of problems?" I ask, turning red-faced.

"On the contrary, it is a much quicker and truthful way to communicate. We have evolved our thinking to be less judgmental and more honest. Not to worry, Hawk. Here, we do not pay attention to appearances," the leader says with a little smile. At least I think it's a smile. His mouth is stretched awkwardly across his thin grey neck.

"Yes, Matt," he sighs, looking at Matt, "that is why our heads are so big.... Big brains."

"But I didn't say..." Matt stammers, "Oh...ESP!" Matt's bronze skin turns red, making his ears glow.

"My name is Yxzyurchmung. Mung the Elder, but you can call me Mung. This is planetoid Shnergla of the solar system Pixa-Utopia," he explains. "How did you come to our land at just the right moment to vanquish the dreaded Booger-Bully drone attacks? And help our people?"

"Well it's a crazy story but..." I start to say.

"Ahhhhh. I see," Mung snorts through the two slits he has for a nose. "The radio wormhole thing again."

"Whaaaaaa...? Oh, you read my mind," I choke out "That is kinda cool! Wait – you've had other visitors through this wormhole?"

"Correct, you are not the first and you will not be the last," replies Mung.

"But how does this wormhole thing work?" Matt asks, scratching his head.

"If you get too close to a wormhole opening, you will be sucked into a quantum gravity propulsion tunnel and hyper-fast interstellar travel," Mung explains.

"Oh, that explains everything!" Matt sighs, looking at me for help.

"We'll talk about it later, Matt." I look at Mung, getting more and more curious about the other wormhole traveler, "How do you know our language? Did the previous visitor teach you?"

"How come our heads didn't explode in outer space?" Matt asks, looking at me as we do a high five.

"Good question, dude!" I was wondering about that myself.

"We understand over one million languages from every intelligent life form in the Multiverse. Our ESP language skills help us detect and identify if a contact is friend or foe. Then we can activate the protective shield," Mung explains, "...and your heads did not explode because we live in an artificially pressurized atmosphere."

Matt and I look at each other, "Cool!" we say at the same time. Like we can't believe we're in outer space, on another planet talking to an actual alien. They really do exist! BAM! That blows our minds!

CHAPTER 6

GALACTIC BULLIES

"Wait, you know of Planet Earth? But why haven't you made contact?" I ask him, trying to wrap my brain around the fact that there are other life forms in outer space. *And* they know *we* exist. *This is huge!*

"Yes, we have watched your planet's evolution," Mung says with his eyes looking down. "Unfortunately, we did not feel Earthlings were ready for alien visitors yet. We monitored transmissions about extraterrestrials on your radio and television shows this past century," Mung states, shaking his large head, "Tsk, tsk. They are so inaccurate, so violent!"

"What about *Star Trekkers*? It's the best show ever!" Matt cries.

"Our planet has our own version of that show called *Star Champions of Peace*, where our squads visit other planets to make friends and teach non violence," Mung explains.

"That's so...!" says Matt, "Umphhh," he gasps as I elbow him. "Ah, I mean, that sounds fun," Matt says, rubbing his arm with a hurt look.

"So how come the drones are terrorizing your planet?" I ask Mung. We walk towards the high-tech alien cityscape looking all around us in wonder. We see grey aliens of different shapes and sizes stop what they're doing and stare at us. Mung lifts his spindly fingers to reassure them...and us.

"The Boogernauties are bullies who raid other planets and take what they need. Like food, clothing, products, and even slaves."

"My Paw told me about slavery of black people on our planet. That's not cool," Matt says sadly.

"That is what the Booger-Bullies want to do to us. We are a peaceful planet and have no weapons. We are an easy target," Mung says. "All we have is our protective cloaking device."

"Sounds like Big Mikey at school," Matt whispers.

"But what do they want from you?" I ask Mung.

"Our planet has infrasound waves, like your music. Which the Boogers want to steal and use for evil purposes," he explains.

"How can they do that?" I wonder.

"We use infrasound at low frequencies to keep Shnerglers relaxed and happy. Positive, inspiring sound waves are piped into the atmosphere and give everyone a sense of peace and well-being." He points to the relaxed community around us with a long-fingered arm. "But the Boogers want to use this technology to turn their own people and their captives into zombies. They will hypnotize and brainwash them with low-frequency sound waves to make them do what they want," Mung explains.

"Whoa, that sounds like the movie I saw last week called *Zombella*," Matt says, darting his eyes around looking for zombies.

"I saw that one too," I exclaim. "Godzilla came out

of the black lagoon and ate all the zombies and…" I stop when I see Mung and the other peaceful aliens shocked expressions, scared that this may happen to them. "Uhh, sorry. Let's stay focused, Matt." Turning to Mung I ask, "Is it playing right now?"

"Yes, it is," Mung says, checking his wrist-screen and rolling his huge eyes back in his oversized head. "Is it not wonderful?" He shivers and looks at us curiously.

"I could use something to calm me down right now, but I don't hear anything. How about you Matt?" I ask.

"Nothing," he says, looking around as if he might see it, "but I wish I could."

"Let me change the pitch so you can hear it." Mung says. He then pulls up the sleeve of his gown revealing a screen embedded in his wrist, which he taps and snorts into. "There, can you…" Mung stops because we are both screaming.

"Whhaaaaahhh," Matt and I yell, holding our ears. "Turn it off, turn it off!"

"Is something wrong?" Mung asks, tapping his wrist again.

"That's the worst thing I've ever heard!" I say, rubbing my ears.

"What is that anyway?" cries Matt. "I thought you said music?"

"I said infrasound. They are intergalactic sounds converted into subliminal, hypnotic vibes. Massive black holes humming, colliding comet gases, and meteorite showers are just some of the infrasound we use," Mung boasts.

"Oh, I thought it was more like galactic fingernails on a chalkboard!" I exclaim.

"It sounded like the *Incredible Hulk* farting in my eardrum!" Matt cries, wiping tears out of his eyes. "That's your music?!"

"I guess Earthlings are not as sensory sensitive as we are!" Mung retorts with a snort and a shake of his balloon head.

CHAPTER 7

WHAT IS JOKES?

"We must take you to She-Shnerg, our leader," says Mung. "She wants to meet you before moonset to discuss the next attack of the Booger-Bullies."

Matt and I look at each other. "The next attack?" I don't know how to tell him that we don't know anything about defeating bullies, especially alien bullies!

"Zzznap, Dweezil! Come forward," Mung motions.

Two aliens about our height step forward with huge heads bowed. They appear younger than the rest, with the same features: large eyes and tiny neck-mouths. "Show our heroes around, then bring them to the main concourse for mass quantity consumption in one nanohour," Mung orders, gliding away.

"Hawk," whispers Matt. "Did he just say what I think he said?"

"I think he said it's time to eat," I answer.

"Oh good," says Matt. "I haven't had a bite in a billion light-years!" Matt laughs at his own joke.

Zzznap and Dweezil look at each other, and then they look at Matt concerned. "Should we take Hero-Matt to the medic?" Zzznap questions.

"You mean a doctor?" I ask them. "Oh, don't worry, Matt likes to tell jokes," I say, as Matt snickers again.

"What is jokes?" Dweezil asks.

"A joke is something funny...to make people laugh," I say. "Don't you have humor here?"

Zzznap and Dweezil still look confused.

"What does an astronaut put on his toast?" I pause, waiting for effect. "Space Jam," I say.

Matt hoots--it's one of his favorite movies.

"How do you get an alien baby to sleep?" I try again. "You rocket."

Matt and I burst out laughing and high five each other, but the two aliens just look at each other and back at us.

"This way, Hero-Hawk, and Hero-Matt," says Zzznap, awkwardly changing the subject. He points a very long finger-thingy and throws down a board for each of us.

"Oh, hey, it's just Hawk and just Matt," I tell them, even though I like the sound of Hero-Hawk.

"Yes, Just-Hawk and Just-Matt, step on your air-boards," instructs Dweezil.

Oh brother! I don't have time to correct him when I find myself on a flying board trying to keep my balance. "Whoa, whoa! How do I slow it down?" I yell, as my board lifts me off the ground. I feel a sudden jolt as the board goes one way and I go the other. I land flat on my back, the wind knocked out of me. "Oooof."

Matt isn't doing much better on his board. "Aaaaaa! Help!" He shouts and puts his arms out for balance to control his hovering board. His feet go up and his head goes down, hitting a mound of dirt; he does a face plant.

"Dweezil, you might add the training handle to the boards for them," suggests Zzznap helpfully.

"Yes, I agree," says Dweezil, adapting the boards by pressing a button. Almost magically, a long handle pops up, and little wings sprout out at each side. "Try it now."

"Wow, air-scooters!" says Matt scrambling to his feet. He jumps on and takes off like a shot. "This is great! I want one of these at home. I'd be the most popular kid in the schoooooolllll! Yippee Ki-Yay!" Matt screams like the Star Trekkers on their hover crafts, as he does a loop-de-loop over a wacky neon purple bush.

"Wait for me, Matt!" I gasp, hopping on my air-scooter and tearing after him. "Woo Hoo! This is better than the Wild Mouse at *Wally World!*" I shout, going as fast as I can to catch up to Matt.

Zzznap and Dweezil try to head us off on their air-boards. "Wait for us, Just-Hawk and Just-Matt! You don't know where to goooooo!" a concerned Zzznap shouts, coming after us.

We dodge them and fly past a school of young, light grey Shnerglets. They stand, linking tentacles and watching us with their neck-mouths hanging open. We wave at them. Then we zoom past a massive red tree with sky-pods hanging from the branches like giant, high-tech bird nests. Little grey faces with big oval eyes look out at us. Alien condos, I wonder, as we streak past one after another, with each of their eyes following us. I look up to see two moons looking down on us from above, like two eyes shining in the bright sky. I slow my board down and see Matt ahead of me doing the same.

We can't believe our eyes. Matt turns to look back at me, his shaky finger pointing up at the moons.

Two moons!

Dweezil and Zzznap catch up to us and hover alongside. "You notice our sacred moons. They give us light and life. Our moons tell us the passage of time as they watch over us. We live on the dark side of the planet, so our moons provide our life-giving light," says Zzznap solemnly, hanging his head before the beautiful full moons.

The realization hits me like a punch to the solar plexus. We're in a tiny galaxy far, far away, on hover-scooters! How are we ever going to get back home? Matt and I always dreamed of being astronauts. I just didn't think it would happen when we were ten years old!

CHAPTER 8

I WON'T HAVE WHAT HE'S HAVING

At the main concourse cafeteria, we see hundreds of food vending machines. All the Shnerglers lining up in order of height, shortest to tallest, wait for their turn at the dispensers. Zzznap explains that they all live together and take care of each other in a communal society. We take our place in line and look around at the beautiful alien dining hall. It's a sky-dome of glass prisms, shooting rainbows of color everywhere with mirrors for a crazy, dazzling effect. It stimulates our eyes and our brains and I've never felt so, so… brainy. Dweezil tells us the rainbows are meant to fill us with joy and love. It works as I suddenly feel really happy …and hungry!

The other aliens are talking and animating to each other. They point a long finger into the spout like a water fountain. "Do you have any cola and milk? I could really go for one right now," I say, and everyone, I mean everyone, in the cafeteria just stops and looks at me like my hair is on fire. I pat my head just in case and shrug.

When it's our turn, Zzznap shows us the three choices for food. "We have interesting nourishment this night. Green button is googash, my favorite – in your language is Shnerg-lizard tongues and livers mixed with goo-grass," Zzznap explains.

Matt and I look at each other and stick our own tongues out.

"Red button is moolatte – the milk mixed with the blood of our moo-beast," he says. Matt and I grab our throats and pretend to puke.

Dweezil adds, "Blue button is shmoodle, in your language it is spaghetti and tennis balls."

"You mean meatballs?" I ask hopefully.

"Correct, meatballs. I jokes you," Dweezil says.

"Ha! Good one, Dweezil!" Matt says, chuckling as we high five each other. "I'll have the blue button!" we both shout, licking our lips.

"Just-Hawk, why do you slap hands in air with Just-Matt?" Dweezil asks.

"It's how friends show they are happy with each other," I explain "Here, try it with Zzznap." I pull them together and put their long-fingered hands up and they try to slap hands but miss. "Wait, you don't want to miss when you high five, that's the worst thing that can happen." *Sheesh, I don't want to teach them how to be 'not cool'.* "Try again. This time do a little jump and slap with confidence."

They do it right this time and Matt and I turn to them and we high five them. "Cool!" Matt says.

We don't even know if they have five. Whatever! We are so excited right now we almost forget that we are light-years from home and hanging out with aliens our age.

Zzznap turns back to the food dispenser. "It is time to consume mass quantities!" he instructs. "Make a selection and stick your long finger in here." Zzznap demonstrates as he presses the green button and sticks his own long tentacle into a nozzle which seals around it. He closes his eyes as he enjoys his googash. *Whoa, that's why their mouths are so tiny...they don't use them to eat!*

Dweezil presses the red button for some moolatte and puts his long finger into the spout. When he realizes we don't have an intake finger, he is unable to help us because he is connected to the nozzle.

I push the blue button in front of me and try to put my mouth on the nozzle, but Zzznap shakes his head.

"No! No, Just-Hawk! Not like that!" he cries trying to reach over to help.

I move my mouth away and shmoodle comes squirting out of the nozzle and sprays Matt from head to toe in what looks like already chewed-up spaghetti and meatballs.

"Yuck! Why'd you have to do that?" Matt yells, looking over at me with mashed noodles all over his surprised face. He looks so funny that I start to laugh. Zzznap's digit pops out of his nozzle right then, with a loud sucking sound and goo spews all over Dweezil.

That's when Matt points the hose right at me and puts his finger on the red button.

"No, Matt! Don't do it!" I scream too late. I get a shot of moolatte in my face and down my shirt! Gross and stinky! *Eeeww!*

"Food-fight!" I yell, picking up my nozzle and pushing a button as Matt ducks, and Zzznap gets shmoodle in both of his huge eyes. "Youch. Just-Hawk, Just-Matt, what are you doing?" he asks, rubbing mush out of his eye sockets.

Little janitor-droids with spray bottles and tiny vacuums attached to them come at us from every direction to clean up the mess. We look at each other in horror as they start pulling off our dirty clothes and wiping us down. "Whoa, Stop that!" I yell trying to cover myself and Matt backs away with his hands up. But they are too fast. Fluttering around us like hummingbirds, the droids keep up their attack until we are all cleaned up and wearing long robes like Dweezil and Zzznap and everyone else in the hall. We look at each other in shock then start to laugh; our hair is all pulled back into man-buns. Matt looks super funny with his afro sculpted into a bun. Luckily, Zzznap and Dweezil have been cleaned up too because there's an announcement over a loudspeaker. We hear a horrible sound like a needle scratched across a turntable. Then Mung's voice booms out, calling for everyone to gather at the front of the main concourse in preparation for She-Shnerg's arrival.

"Ooooooohhhh," I groan as I suddenly feel sick. I want to go home.

CHAPTER 9

THE SHE-SHNERG

We can feel the tension in the room grow as all the Shnerglers seem anxious and excited at the same time. The aliens are using telepathy, so everything is silent except for the odd buzzing sound in the hall. It's very low, like a vibration we can feel. Matt and I look all around at the Shnerglers who are shivering and vibrating and, and...buzzing. The vibrations get stronger and the buzz gets louder, like the theremin solo from our favorite show.

"Sounds like *Star Trekkers!*" Matt whispers all excited.

I guess She-Shnerg doesn't make many public appearances.

We are caught up in the excitement of this rock band entrance when we hear a commotion outside the hall opening. She-Shnerg appears, and She is awesome! She's at least ten feet tall, with huge almond-shaped black eyes, tiny mouth, and grey skin. A shock of white hair cascades behind her as she glides across the concourse. On her shoulder perches a beautiful bird-like creature. It has long tail feathers of red and gold, and looks like the fiery phoenix from Greek mythology Mrs. Bupkiss showed us. A halo glows like sunlight around both of them.

She bows and raises two long arms in the air for quiet. "Greetings, friends and visitors. Thank you for that exciting welcome."

She-Shnerg is beautiful but frightening, and so is her bird. Its beady eyes stare right into us. Matt and I watch everyone around us, looking for a sign. Should we be nervous or worried? Will She help us get home?

Zzznap reads my mind and explains, "She-Shnerg is so tall because she is the last remaining member of the Gigantes, the first ones to teach us how to live peacefully. The Gigantes never stop growing, so the chief-elders were the tallest. She outlived and outgrew them all. The creature on her shoulder is her spirit-mate and most important advisor, Kismet. He has cosmic power. He reads the stars and sees our planet's destiny. He predicted your arrival here as the 'Worm-Ones', and foretold of your help with the Boogers."

The Worm-Ones! Matt and I look at each other, eyebrows raised. "You're a worm, Hawk!" whisper-chuckles Matt.

I point at him, 'No, you are!' But I am dazed and confused: *how did Kismet know we were coming?* I am taken aback by this revelation and have to shake my head to clear it. *Maybe we should ask Kismet how to get back home!*

She-Shnerg raises her long, graceful arms. "This is a proud moment for all Shnerglers. We peacefully stood up to another attack of the Booger-Bullies. Your kindness and compassion in the face of our aggressors is what our society is built upon. Love our neighbor and a peaceful resolution will be the reward. Yes?" she states, as the vibrations and buzzing in the room rise again. We watch as She-Shnerg heads over to a large chair with a built-in perch for Kismet. Mung approaches her and bows as She takes a seat. He nods and then motions us forward.

Matt and I grab for each other and walk slowly and shakily towards She-Shnerg.

Suddenly I hear a soft voice in my head. It says, "Do not be afraid, Hawk. Welcome to our planetoid. We have been waiting for you for a long time."

I get chills down my spine and I am shocked that She is talking to me inside my brain! I look around, panicked, and we make eye contact.

"Yes, it is I, Hawk," She-Shnerg says.

I go red and try to clear my thoughts.

"Our citizens wish to thank you for your bravery and skills in defeating the Booger attack drones. We wish to bestow on you our highest honor by making you official members of the Star Champions of Peace. The S.C.P.," announces She-Shnerg.

Mung comes forward to put a silver badge on our chests, as the Shnerglers start vibrating and buzzing again. I look at it, but I cannot read it.

"Um, thank you She-Shnerg," I say shyly, still shaky. "We are honored and don't want to offend, but we need your help to return to our home planet, Earth. We know there was another visitor through the wormhole. Can you tell me who that was and how they left your planetoid?"

"We must wait for that discussion. First we must deal with a more pressing problem. Kismet says the Boogernauties are very angry and are planning a revenge attack for the loss of their drones." She continues, "As members of the S.C.P. you must help us to peacefully overcome the Booger-Bullies." After She-Shnerg gives her command, she has a conversation with Kismet that we can't hear.

"But, but, Matt and I have to get back to our own planet! Our own country! Our own clubhouse!" I blurt out desperately looking over at Matt and Mung for help.

"Ya sorry, but I have a dentist appointment tomorrow," Matt says shaking his man-bun back and forth. You can really make a point with a man-bun.

"It may be possible to send you back to Earth once the Cosmic Boogers have all been picked off!" Mung adds, tapping his wrist with a long finger.

Matt stifles his laughter and I shoot him a 'Can we be serious' look.

"How can we do anything against a whole army of Booger-Bullies?" I ask in disbelief.

I feel guilty that we got the Boogers angry in the first place by destroying their drones. But if we hadn't shown up, they could all be slaves right now. It occurs to me that I won't be able to focus on getting back home when I know that the Boogers are planning another raid on this peaceful planet and our new friends.

"What do you say, Matt, should we help?" I ask looking at him.

"Let's do this partner. I don't like going to the dentist anyway," he says, as we do our space club handshake.

CHAPTER 10

RAMBOOGER RAMS IN

W e sit at a long table with She-Shnerg, Mung, Matt and Kismet. We watch a large screen showing the worried faces of all the little Shnerglers. Their huge heads droop like deflated helium balloons.

She-Shnerg raises her arms for attention. "Kismet says we will arrange for your return trip to Earth after you help us find a peaceful resolution to the Boogernaut threat." She looks at me and Matt expectantly.

Matt raises his hand like he's in school. "I just thought of something cool from *Star Trekkers*. We can build a giant catapult and hit them with massive moon pies! They'll eat some of the moon pies and want more so they'll be like your BAFFs," Matt says, trying to high five me as I look around at the scowling faces of the Shnerglers.

"Um, Matt that worked against the Sugar-Demons of Saturn but it's a little too aggressive. And what are BAFFs anyways?" I ask.

"Best Alien Friends Forever! It could work!" he shrugs.

"Let's think of something a little more peaceful," I say.

Mung rolls his enormous eyes, and says, "*Star Trekkers*," and goes on to explain how we might return home. "When we reopen the wormhole, we can use a stasis-field Ray-bobble to fling you and Matt across the space-time abyss, back to Earth," he says with a snort of confidence we don't feel.

"Hawk, bobble-fling, what did he...?" Matt looks at me, confused.

"He said we could go back home the same way we came here," I tell Matt. Then I turn to Mung, "Wait, did you say Ray-bobble?"

"Yes, Hawk," the She-Shnerg's voice says in my head. "We invented a 'bobble-enclosure', protected with a stasis-field and named it after another young Earthling who came to our planet some time ago." She continues, "He too, needed help getting home."

"My Grandpa's name was Ray, and it's his radio that brought us here." Matt and I look at each other with our mouths hanging open. Can it be my Grandpa was here when he was young? I shake my head as all the pieces fall into place in my mind. *My Grandpa did this too!*

"Kismet has foretold it. You and Matt will help us devise a plan to appease the Boogernauties," Mung declares.

"I suggest you go to the Hall of Truth to find a peaceful solution to the Booger problem. You may also find there some of the answers you seek," states She-Shnerg, as a look of approval passes between She and Mung.

Suddenly a loud siren starts blasting in everyone's ears, followed by: "Danger, Danger!"

The screen in front of us changes from the main concourse full of little Shnerglers to a disgusting looking black and green mutant insect or humanoid. He is wheezing heavily and drooling everywhere, and looks pretty angry.

"Well isn't this a fun party! (wheeze) All the top brass of Shnergla, together at last. (wheeze) She-Tree, Mung-the-tung, and of course Kismet; the cosmic-waste-of-space. (wheeze-cackle-wheeze) I guess my invitation got lost in the stratosphere? Are these the foul creatures that destroyed our explorer drones?" he wheezes, looking at Matt and me with a sneer and a drool.

"Hey, didn't we see him on an episode of *Star Trekkers*? 'Java the Butt'!" Matt whispers to me.

I elbow him to be quiet before he gets us killed. "Shhhh!"

"Now, RamBooger, you cannot crash our meeting and be rude. We will not stand for it," says Mung forcefully, wagging a spindly finger.

"Well sit down then, because I have a message for you," RamBooger roars, spewing saliva. Mung sinks into his hammock, speechless. Matt and I cling onto each other. "You have until moonrise to give us what we want or we're going to blow your protective shield AND your tiny planet out of this galaxy! (gasp-wheeze) After we take what's coming to us of course." RamBooger starts to laugh, a terrifying wheezy-cackle. "Mwahahaha-snort" Then the screen flicks back to show the little Shnerglers in the concourse with their hands on either side of their open neck-mouths; like an alien version of the famous painting 'The Scream.'

CHAPTER 11

HALL OF TRUTH

Zzznap, Dweezil, Matt and I have been given instructions to go to the Great Hall of Truth to research ways to deal with the Boogernaut threat. She-Shnerg said it may also be my chance to learn the truth about the wormhole and the last Earthling to make a surprise visit to this Planetoid. I need to know if it was my Grandpa. It would explain a lot of things: his love of space, his crazy radio... *Could it be what he wanted to share with me was that he was a space traveler?*

"Wowwww," Matt and I whisper because it feels like we're in an awesome library. It's the most beautiful library I've ever seen. A super-duper wonder of art and glass, like never seen before on Earth. A glass dome ceiling, so high we can't see the end of it, vaults spaceward. Twinkling stars and two moons light up the purple sky of the incredible galaxy above us.

"Whoa, feels like we're in a giant bubble in space!" marvels Matt, looking up in awe.

I start to feel dizzy because it looks so different from our night sky. No Big Dipper or Orion's Belt here. I don't recognize any of these constellations. Gargoyles and other-worldly creatures are carved into the giant beams and columns that hold up the glass structure. Massive screens of what looks like hieroglyphics – maybe Shnergla text, line the walls and light up the room.

The image of the running text runs across our stunned faces as we look skyward. Strangely, I immediately feel smarter in this great hall; like the information is going directly into my brain. It's like I'm thinking things I never thought of before, like: Is this universe for real? Maybe because my grandpa is on my mind, I wonder if we become part of the cosmos when we die. I look at Matt to see if he notices anything weird, but he's looking up with his mouth hanging open.

Zzznap decides to download the Boogernaut data and tell us what happened to make them so wicked. It turns out Boogernaut was once a peaceful planet, led by the Gigantes, She-Shnerg's long-ago ancestors. But they were overthrown by a war-loving clan with their drones and elite fighters called the Booger-Bullies or BBs. Led by commander RamBullish, they terrorized Boogernaut and expelled the Gigantes, who escaped to Planetoid Shnergla. The Gigantes eventually became Shnergla's chief-elders and leaders. The rest of the population of Boogernaut was taken over by RamBullish and later by RamBooger's bullies. The most aggressive young ones were recruited to the BBs and taught to be cruel and ruthless. They grew up to be true bullies and terrorized and oppressed the rest of the planet. The BBs use brutality to keep the Boogernauts in line and drone attacks to take over other planets and kidnap the inhabitants to turn them into slaves.

"Their anthem is 'Bully them one, bully them all, bully them all until they fall!' Tsk, Tsk, so barbaric!" sighs Zzznap.

Dweezil uses his wrist monitor to link up with the

supercomputer and locate their data on Planet Earth. We see unfamiliar symbols flash by on the screens as he downloads information, monitoring the tiny screen embedded in his wrist. Dweezil speaks of learning about Earth's great leaders--My Hat Gandi, King Martin II, and BeatleJohn. When he explains their greatness, I laugh and tell him its Mahatma Gandhi, Martin Luther King Jr. and John Lennon of 'The Beatles'--our great peace leaders.

"If only they could help us," Zzznap exclaims wistfully. "We must take this data to She-Shnerg and Kismet so they can figure out how to stop this reign of bullies."

"Wait Zzznap, The Supreme Leader said I would find out more about the other visitor who came through the wormhole. Can we look it up?" I plead.

"OK, I will access Earth alien and wormhole," replies Zzznap.

"What does it say?" I beg Zzznap.

"It says an Earthling named Ray came through a wormhole that was created at the Chicxulub crater when there was a large meteor strike millions of years earlier," explains Zzznap.

"Ray, that was my grandfather's name. But Mung said he used the wormhole radio?" I probe.

"The data documents that he was in Mexico for the solar eclipse of the century in Earth time 1970. He fell with his radio into a cenote, or hole in the ground at the crater site."

"I don't see what the radio has to do with it," I puzzle.

"It is recorded that they went through this cenote

together, and the radio developed the ability to reopen the wormhole. That is how you were able to use it to come here," continues Zzznap.

"You mean the radio became like, radio-active?" quips Matt.

"Good one Matt. Yes, that is correct--it is an active wormhole," affirms Zzznap.

"My Grandpa had a portal to space! And he came to Shnergla too!" I cry looking at Matt.

"Wow your Grandpa was the coolest, Hawk! My Grandpapa was a farmer, so the only wormholes he had were in his apples!" jokes Matt.

Dweezil interrupts, "We should go back now, She-Shnerg will be waiting for us," he says, hurrying us to the monorail and back to the main concourse.

CHAPTER 12

TRO-JOHN HORSE

As we fly through the night in a high-speed capsule, back to our pods, I keep thinking about John Lennon's song "Give Peace a Chance". My dad is a big Beatles fan, so I had to listen to his music all the time. Even though I would beg him to put on 'The Gorillaz' instead, I'm glad he didn't listen to me. Staring out across the universe something shoots into my brain like a quasar. I realize that John Lennon's message of peace was an inspiration for the aliens on this planet, and they thought of him as a great leader. As the song spills out in my head, I blurt out, "Eureka!!"

Matt looks at me surprised, "What does that mean?"

"It's Greek for I found a solution!" I say getting excited. "Instead of using the infrasound message to make the Boogers into zombies, we'll use a message that encourages them all back to a peaceful way of life." I look around, but they aren't following, "It could even work on the dreaded BBs--like a Trojan Horse." I jump up and down and slap my forehead. "Matt, remember the story Mrs. Bupkiss read to us about the Greek city of Troy and the huge wooden horse. It was given as a gift, but the huge hollow horse was filled with soldiers ready to surprise and defeat Troy's army. The Boogers will think that we're giving them what they want to turn their citizens into zombie-slaves. But we will surprise them with a message of love and peace with John Lennon's song lyrics. What a bombshell!"

"Yeah!" exclaims Matt, rubbing his hands together. "The good message could be hidden behind the bad message, and we slam them with it when they least expect it. Bam!"

"Totally, dude!" I shout as we high five and then high five Zzznap and Dweezil. "If it works, we'll be on our way back to Earth in time for pizza!"

When we see She-Shnerg, she exclaims "It is a wonderful plan...and Kismet agrees. It just may work." She has already read our thoughts, and She communicates to everyone how it will work. I'm still getting used to this ESP stuff. When She explains, it's like I already know what She is going to say. We are connected telepathically, and her words are like an echo in my head. It's a creepy feeling and my hair stands on end at this weird sensation. Feeling naked and exposed, I try to build a mental wall to hide my thoughts behind. I wonder if she knows how sad I am about my Grandpa.

She-Shnerg continues, "We will program the transmitter with duo-emission, so that it can emit two separate frequencies of infrasound. One with the enslaving message, and the other with a subliminal message of tolerance and peace". She explains further, "The first message will be the one they are expecting, to make slaves of the Boogernauties. And the hidden frequency will be a hypnotic message of peace and friendship for everyone, including the BBs".

She-Shnerg tells us it may take a few micro-planet orbits to complete the transformation. But, if it works, it could stop the drone attacks for good and save the Boogernauties from becoming zombie-slaves.

"Um Hawk, what did she just...?" asks Matt, looking from one face to another.

"We're going to spring a peace-attack on them. Let's do this!" I say high fiving everyone.

Secretly, I'm praying that it works. Then we can focus on getting back to our home planet, where we don't have to worry about scary, drooling, alien monsters who want to blow us up!

CHAPTER 13

WHAT'S THE FREQUENCY, MUNG?

The concourse is abuzz with excitement as everyone prepares for RamBooger's expected big-screen appearance and the beginning of our plan. Matt and I look at each other nervously. If this plan doesn't work out, we may never get home....or worse we'll become Booger zombie-slaves! Mung and his group of elders did the remix of the two frequencies of infrasound to hand over to the Bullies. The good message includes John Lennon's "Give Peace a Chance" lyrics, as well as inspiring words from Martin Luther King's "I Have a Dream" speech. It's a double dose of love and respect for their naughty neighbors.

Suddenly, a siren explodes in our ears, as a sneering RamBooger appears on the screens all around the concourse. Larger than life, drooling and wheezing, he looks like something out of my worst nightmare. He is even more menacing now, wearing his armor and surrounded by his army of BBs holding weapons.

"Time's up, losers! (wheeze) What's it going to be, Tree?" RamBooger jeers, addressing She-Shnerg. "Cooperate with us, (wheeze) or DEATH?" he demands, as saliva spews out across the screen in front of him and slides down into small puddles. RamBooger raises his claw-like hand and the BBs behind him aim their weapons at the camera. The effect in the concourse is terrifying for the peaceful Shnerglers--a hundred screens of armed BBs surround us.

"It doesn't seem like a difficult (wheeze-gasp) choice to me." RamBooger licks his lips and shows us his greenish-brown teeth then picks up a rocket launcher for full effect. He's getting his message across, loud and clear. Matt was right, he does look like Java the Butt...and acts like him too.

"You are correct, RamBooger," She-Shnerg says with confidence. "We are a peaceful planet and we do not desire war with you. We have prepared the Sound-Energy Flux device for you and the BBs to use as you requested. In return we require a peace treaty from you that we hope you will respect and expect that you will spare our humble planet any more grief?" She bows and turns away to confer with Kismet.

"For best results, we advise that you pipe it directly into the atmosphere. That way everyone will hear it and be inspired to follow all your commands," Mung adds, his huge eye seems to wink at me.

A scowling RamBooger accepts the deal but looks disappointed that he won't get to blow us all up. Then the screen goes black.

"The S.C.P. will deliver the device and get a guarantee of a cease-fire treaty in return," declares Mung. "Hawk and Matt, you will accompany them to ensure everything goes according to plan."

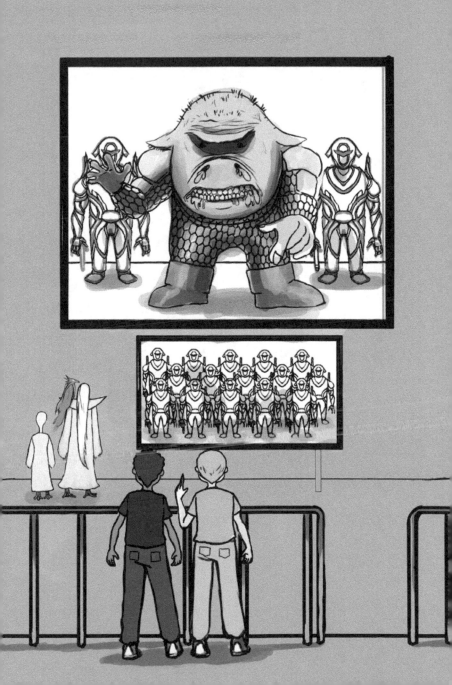

CHAPTER 14

GIVE PEACE A CHANCE

RamBooger wastes no time activating the infrasound program to create more slave-zombies and get them to work harder. Mung and the Elders monitor the situation on Planet Boogernaut and the rest of us watch the action play out on the big screens. We hope our Trojan horse will be a success so that we can make a plan to go home. *All this talk of love is making me feel homesick!* At first, it is working the way RamBooger hopes, with the Boogernauties surrendering to the slave message and becoming very zombie-like. Then She-Shnerg switches the emission frequency, and the 'Give Peace a Chance' message begins to circulate. We notice a difference in the society as we watch the screens. They hum the peace tune mantra as they go about their chores. Smiling slaves ignore orders from the BBs – and nothing happens! The BBs don't punish them. There is no reaction to suggest they are bothered by these acts of rebellion. With each broadcast, the cooperation and consideration shown by the Boogernauties to each other increases. A free society is being created in front of our eyes! Boogernauties are becoming free: free to be happy, free to grow food and free to enjoy it with their fellow-Boogers. But the big question is: How will RamBooger react?

And there it is! RamBooger seems indifferent to the rebellion of those he meant to be slaves. Joy spreads throughout the land as the BBs join the 'Peace' revolution. Now not just the captives and slaves but the bullies, too, are singing the peace mantra and repeating the lyrics. From time to time a small conflict breaks out but mostly it's a picture of harmony. I'd have said that peaceful co-existence between these guys was impossible but look! Boogernauties and BBs smiling at each other, and having sing-alongs. *Imagine all the BBs, living life in peace.* John Lennon lives on, light-years from Liverpool where his life began and New York where it ended.

A BB reaches out to share the load of someone who moments ago was a slave. Then another does it...and another, and now even RamBooger has laid down his weapon and picked up a pallet. The heaviest pallet, of course, he being the strongest Booger in sight. Everyone is working happily together.

A few micro-planet orbits later, RamBooger arranges a video-contact with She-Shnerg. He thanks her for her wisdom and the wonderful gift of peace and love she has given them.

"Greetings She-Shnerg and my apologies to all Shnerglers for my past behavior," RamBooger says, wheezing and crying, "I want to thank you for the gift you have given us (wheeze-sob). Boogernaut is a wonderful place to co-exist with our friends, now that we all work together...and play together." He sobs and I almost feel sorry for him. He wipes his eyes with a tissue then snorts a large booger into it. *Eeew gross!* Matt and I look at each other and grimace.

"I never knew it could feel so powerful to be loved and give love in return. (blubber-sniff)...Nobody ever loved me before!" He sobs (wheeze-waaah).

Sheesh! I've heard of ugly crying, but this is the ugliest crying I've ever seen!

"I have to go now, to help plan our First Annual Booger Peace Fest and where we will premiere our new national anthem. (sniff-wheeze-gasp) I was inspired with some beautiful words and I don't even know how they came to me. This is all so exciting, and we owe it all to you!" RamBooger bows and blows his nose like the sound of an elephant trumpeting. "I want to extend an invitation and hope your leaders and the Earthlings can join us in our celebration. We are planning a great peace-loving event and you are all most welcome!" He signs off with a flourish of spittle, drool and tears.

CHAPTER 15

THE BOOGER PEACE FEST

Matt and I are super excited, because we are going to the Booger Peace Fest. Ahem! We are traveling first class, with She-Shnerg and Mung, to Planet Boogernaut. Imagine! Us, in first class! They usher us into a tiny rocket ship and help us into a comfy pressurized spacesuit.

"Woohoo this is awesome!" shouts Matt. "Our first ride in a spaceship!" Matt is over the moon, and our spacesuits are just like the ones on *Star Trekkers*! Mine has a built-in screen for watching videos, or the rocket-cam outside. There are so many buttons; one for food, one for liquids and even one for helping us go to the bathroom. We've never imagined a first class like this! Mung is bringing us to their Coliseum for the festivities as instructed on the invitation.

The Coliseum is a massive stadium with a large figure 8-shaped track, where teams whiz around the track on air boards. The two planets share a love of these 'hover-board' games, but the Shnergla team is teaching the Boogernauties how to make it a team sport, rather than a competition. Both planets are engaged in a friendly relay of the first 'Air-Runner Duo-Planet Cup'. The teams are tearing around the track so fast that Matt and I get dizzy trying to follow them. We can't believe how fast they are going.

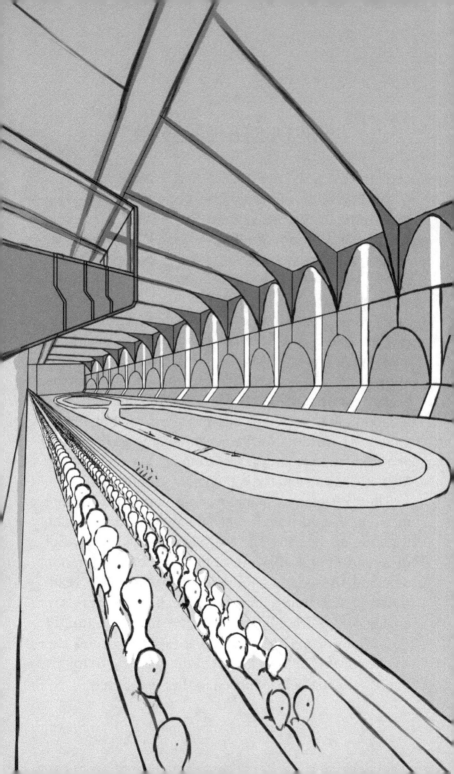

"Mung, who is going to win?" I ask.

"Ya, who are you going to bet on?" Matt adds. "And can we get some popcorn?"

Mung is confused at first, but then he understands. "Oh yes, winning and beating the opposition is Earth's way," he replies. "On Shnergla, we do things differently, it is not about competition; it is about teamwork."

"So, they're all on the same team?" Matt quizzes, popping some alien snacks into his mouth. He makes a weird face and looks in the container to see it's popped lizard eyeballs. "Ugh! What's with the lizard food here!" he croaks.

"Our protein is simulated lizard meat. We would never consume another living being on our planet!" Mung looks repulsed even at the idea of such a thing. He sighs then continues, "The elite air runners from each planet work together to help each other go faster," Mung explains, "We call them air runners because they go faster by running on the airwaves generated by their teammates. The goal is not to beat the others on the track, but to generate greater and greater airwave energy to push each other forward around the track."

"But what are the goals and how do they win?" I ask.

"Our team races against the clock to go faster and break the best time by building on their skills," Mung exclaims. "They hope to break their record tonight." He rubs his tentacled hands together in anticipation.

"Are they racing now?" Matt queries.

"This is just the warm-up, the race starts after the leaders arrive," Mung says, never taking his eyes off the track.

When RamBooger and She-Shnerg arrive, there is great excitement with much quivering and vibrating in the arena. RamBooger blows the 'Interplanetary Cup' horn to declare the start of the games and gasps, winded from the effort. "(wheeze) Thank you Boogernauties and Shnerglers (gasp-wheeze) and welcome to the first ever Booger Peace Fest. (snort-gasp) We have an exciting air runners competition planned and then a great feast will follow. (wheeze-cough) Before we start the games we would like to present the first performance of our new anthem of peace. (cough-splutter-snort)," he declares.

The screens around the arena light up and a slide show flashes across them of how their society has improved; little boogies helping older boogernauties, and all of them working, singing, dancing and playing together. The images jump from one screen to the next and race around the arena; so we are surrounded by their message of love and kindness. All in the stadium stand up and put their green claws on their chests and chant, "No more pushing, no more fighting, Boogers now are all uniting. No more wars, no more slaying, peace and love is all we are saying." She-Shnerg raises her long arms, and the Shnerglers in the stands start to do their buzzing-theremin melody to go along with the Boogers repeated chants. RamBooger was right, the words are perfect, and it becomes a very powerful anthem. As it comes to an end, the whole arena erupts into stamping of tentacles and quivering.

"I think it's going to be a hit," I tell Matt.

I look over at RamBooger to see he's overcome with tears and snot again as She-Shnerg tries to comfort him.

At last, they stand together, holding hands as She makes an announcement, "That was inspiring and a perfect way to begin our new relationship of working together, and our interplanetary games. Let the first Inter-Planet Air-Runner Cup begin! And may both teams win!" Bowing down, they cause the crowd to quiver and quake with incredible joy and excitement. The two teams take their places.

Mung tells us that the two teams will run alongside each other and each help the other team to go faster. This is new for the Boogers, as they would normally try to slow the other team down. In their newfound interplanetary spirit of peace, they are excited to try this new style of teamwork.

A loud pop signals the start of the race and off they go!

Large timers and speedometers at either end of the stadium show the time elapsed, the velocity of each team, and the number of laps left. The high-speed air runners and the crowd take quick looks at the clock as they round the corners. All heads move in unison from the runners to the clocks to see if their time is fast enough to break the record.

Air runners zoom forward or fall back at different points along the track with clock-like precision. Each runner pushes the other forward, until it's time for them to fall back.

The crowd stands up as it's clear this is going to be a tight race. All Shnergler and Booger fans begin to rock in a circular motion, so their kinetic energy helps move the teams along. With two laps remaining, the crowd is cheering and rocking so hard it seems the stadium will collapse. Both teams are going for it and the whole stadium knows it.

"What's happening, Mung?" I shout to be heard over the hum and thump of tentacles.

"It is very close, and even more interesting with the Boogers involved! Both teams are trying to break their records before the other," Mung splutters in his excitement. Suddenly, on the final lap as they round the last corner, the Shnergler team leader notices that the leading Booger is about to fall off his board. Without slowing down, she veers over next to him and steadies him on his board before he falls. They cross the finish line together in a dead heat, tied, as they raise their hands over their heads in victory. They both look over at the scoreboard to see that they each shattered their old records, and the whole stadium goes wild. Streamers and confetti litter the air as the fans stamp their tentacles and congratulate each other.

"Wow that was awesome!" Matt says giving me a high five.

The excitement continues until RamBooger and She-Shnerg stand up to address the crowd, and everyone quiets down.

RamBooger starts, "That was an amazing victory. Congratulations to both of our Air-runner teams for today's brilliant race! (wheeze-gasp) They both broke their best time records and are proof that working together is good for both teams and may I say for both Planets (snort)."

The crowd jumps up and down vibrating.

Then She-Shnerg nodding says, "I agree, RamBooger! It shows that we are stronger and better together! And now I would like to introduce the next race. The sideboard runs with our juvenile air-runner teams, as well as the newest members of the S.C.P., Hawk and Matt from Planet Earth!"

As the crowd cheers and stomps, Matt looks at me in shock. "What?..."

"Umm, Hawk? Did she just say...?"

CHAPTER 16

I'LL RACE YOU

"**B**e sure to encourage our youngest athletes, (gasp-drool) and our guests from Planet Earth," RamBooger shouts, coughs and wheezes. He sits down next to She-Shnerg, who is smiling and nodding her impressive head in our direction.

"I think I know who arranged this," I tell Matt.

Mung explains that sideboard runs are for future air runners to get used to high speeds and teamwork. In these races, young Shnerglets and Boogies will be placed on sideboards, attached to mainboards, ridden by experienced air runners.

"Why us?" croaks Matt, his voice breaking.

Mung calmly tells us, "You have to represent your planet, Earthlings. Besides Zzznap and Dweezil told us how adept you are on the air-scooters!" He snorts, shaking his balloon head.

Just then six little Shnerglets and Boogies run up to us and drag us by the arms down to the track. They help us put on the aerodynamic suits and helmets and then belt us onto sideboards. I'm thankful that they use protective gear!

One of the Shnerglets shows us her tentacle fingers, as she counts down the rules, "Lean into the curves, do not fall off and most of all, have fun!" Flashing her awkward neck smile, she high fives us then runs over to join the other sideboard. *Our high fives seem to be catching on.*

I look around at all the air runners lined up, ready to fly.

Ohhh, I don't feel so well.

Before I can wave to Mung, I hear a loud pop, my head snaps back and we're off. At first, I am terrified and keep my eyes squeezed shut. Then I start to get into the rhythm of the race. I lean hard from side to side as the boards change curve directions on the figure-8 track. Although not as fast as the first race, the sideboards are the fastest vehicles we've ever been on. We must have been going over 100 mph, as we round the track 20 times. I feel the pressure of acceleration as if I am on the roller-coaster at *Wally World* with all the excitement and rush of adrenaline. We fly around the track so fast that I have trouble keeping up with the curves, but I can't stop smiling.

Each lap, Matt yells, "Yippee Ki-Yay" and the number of times his board finishes first. He shouts out ten on the second to last lap, while I am at nine. I lean in as hard as I can for the final lap and with just ten feet to go, my runner whizzes ahead of Matt's, riding his airwave to the finish line.

I look back at Matt and I croak, "Ten, it's a tie."

The crowd is enjoying our race even more because there is no pressure about breaking records. Just pure fun! We stagger off the track and back into the stands, laughing excitedly, trying to get our land legs back. Our smiles are plastered to our faces from the air pressure.

"I see you enjoyed the sideboard runs," Mung snorts as we join him.

"It was amazing; I've never gone so fast in my life!" I say shaking my head, my blond hair all over the place.

"And you just barely tied me at the end," exclaims Matt, high fiving me.

"Just remember it is about working together, not winning," Mung reminds us, sniffing through his nose slits.

Suddenly, She-Shnerg's voice booms out, "The Peace Fest was an extremely positive start to our newfound friendship and alliance. We hope to hold the second 'Air-Runner Interplanetary Cup' on our planetoid. You are all welcome!" The crowd vibrates and stamps their tentacles in approval.

RamBooger has an announcement also, "I want to invite everyone to join us for mass quantity consumption in the feasting hall (drool). Let us all partake of nourishment as neighbors and friends." RamBooger blows the 'Interplanetary Cup' horn three times to signal the end of the games.

We will never forget this incredible, most amazing day, ever!

CHAPTER 17

GOODBYES

Matt and I are ready to teleport back home. As we travel by air-scooter for one last ride with Zzznap and Dweezil, we are sad to leave them, but excited and nervous about the journey ahead of us. We take the long trip over to the wormhole where Mung and She-Shnerg are waiting for us. We zoom across the alien terrain, over craters, rolling red hills and the scene of the drone attack with debris still littered all over the sand.

"Can I take my air-scooter back with me, Dweezil?" Matt pleads with him again.

"I do not think so, Just-Matt," Dweezil says, blinking his big eyes "It is a very small wormhole."

"Come on, guys, I'll race you to the red rock! Yippee Ki-Yayyy!" Matt screams like we're real Star Trekkers.

As we get to the rock, Dweezil says, "Why are Shnergla's rocks the tastiest?" He pauses for effect, "They are meteor!" he says, looking around for our reactions. We all burst out laughing at Dweezil's joke, and his "human humor". Dweezil and Zzznap high five each other at the same time Matt and I do.

"Ok, Hawk and Matt, let's get serious, now," tuts Mung and we all realize that this may be the last time we see each other.

I look at Matt and we take off our club rings at the same time, as we planned earlier. I hold out my ring to Zzznap and Matt holds his ring out to Dweezil. "Here, guys. We want you to have these to remember us by," I say. "And if there are any more cosmic drone attacks... well, you know what to do."

They take the rings and slide them onto their super-long finger-thingies. "Thank you, Just-Hawk and Just-Matt. We will always remember," they say, high fiving us and doing our secret clubhouse handshake as we taught them.

"She-Shnerg," I say turning towards her, "What can you tell me about my Grandpa Ray?" I start to get a little emotional, my voice cracking. "It's really important that I know more about him."

"We were very fortunate to have our time with Earthling Ray. He was a special young man who showed us that Earthlings are intelligent and tolerant beings. We all loved him so much that when he said he wanted to go home, we built him a 'Bobble' to teleport him back to Earth."

"Yes, he was very special, I miss him so much," I say, feeling like I want to cry for what I lost. "Sometimes I wonder if he meant for me to find the radio, so I could have this experience. He said he wanted to share something important with me, this must have been it. But if he had told me about this before, I may not have believed him." I hang my head, my voice starting to shake.

"We were never sure if he made it home safely. Our data showed there was a problem with the protective stasis-field. But you are living proof that he did indeed survive the trip and led a long and full life on Earth," She answers with a bow of her beautiful great head, with Kismet on her shoulder, bowing too.

"I know this sounds crazy, but knowing he was here, and that he went through the wormhole like we did, makes me feel close to him again, like he's with me now. This whole experience has expanded my mind and I understand now that he'll always be with me. He's part of this whole cosmic universe and so am I," I say smiling and wiping away my tears of joy.

"You are a sensitive and intelligent young person Hawk. Just like your Grandpa." She looks at Kismet and then says, "Kismet says your grandpa is very proud of you."

I look at the mystical Kismet and say, "Can you tell my Grandpa that I love him, and I'll never forget what he taught me."

Smiling and looking from Kismet to me, She-Shnerg says, "You just did."

We are all laughing and crying as She tells us, "I left you and Matt a small gift to remember us by, Hawk. Use it well."

"Thank you, She-Shnerg," I say, with a loud sniff. "We'll never forget either."

"Luckily, we have worked out the bugs in our stasis-field since that time. You two should not have any problems," Mung adds, to bring us back to the present task.

"I think we're ready," I say, looking at Matt for confidence.

"Call 9-1-1; call the Star Trekkers -- Just joking!" Matt says, a nervous smile making his face crumble.

"Climb into the Hawk-Matt Bobble and prepare to be flung....by Mung," snorts Mung making a little joke of his own.

"Cool name," I say, climbing into the bobble that looks like the tilt-a-whirl ride at *Wally World.* I put on my seatbelt and Matt does the same. We wave as the bobble closes on us. I try to reassure Matt. "The trip will be easier in this bobble, bud. L-l-let's j-j-just p-p-pretend we're on the t-t-tilt-a-whirl ride," I shout, with my voice vibrating as we tilt and spin. Then with a surprising blast of power, we are sucked into the wormhole at light speed. We spin backward through the time-space abyss like the tilt-a-whirl car on overdrive.

Matt nods then closes his eyes as the noise and light levels rise to a fever pitch. The wormhole shrinks and expands as cool flames lick at our bobble. I faint as the pressure becomes too much.

EPILOGUE

I wake up to find myself on our clubhouse couch with drool on my shirt. Looking around, I see Matt on the other end of the couch still asleep. I breathe a sigh of relief, "Yes! It was all just a dream! Thank the stars. Next time I won't eat so much moon pie and rocket candies before bed. Talk about your crazy sugar dreams!" I say as I reach over to wake Matt up. When I hear from the garage:

Beep, beep, beep,...

Stay Tuned to Black Hole Radio!

AUTHOR'S NOTE

As a children's librarian in an elementary school, I always wanted to write a story of my own. I got the idea for this book when my children's great uncle died and I ended up with a lot of his belongings in my garage as storage. We heard a beeping coming from the garage on different occasions all summer and finally located the source in a box. It was a small radio with an antenna and it kept beeping at the same time every day, no matter what we did, we couldn't stop the beeping. It was an eerie experience and sparked my imagination to write this story. So you should always be on the lookout for inspiration for a story, you never know when or where it will come from.

GLOSSARY OF SPACE AND SCIENCE TERMS

Antennae: Metal rods for radiating or receiving radio waves (some insects have them).

Astrophysicist: Scientists studying the physical nature of stars and other celestial bodies.

Atmosphere: Gases surrounding a star or planet held in place by gravity.

Barbaric: Savagely cruel, very brutal.

Black hole: It is a region of space where matter has collapsed in on itself.

Comet: A chunk of ice and dust with a long tail orbit a curved path around a planet or star.

Communal: Something that is used or shared by everyone in a group.

Constellation: A group of stars that make up imaginary patterns in the night sky, such as an animal or mythological God.

Cosmic: Relating to the universe or cosmos.

Cosmologist: An astronomer who studies the history of space-time relating to the universe.

Crater: A large hole in the ground on the surface of a planet or moon.

Drone: A flying robot that can be remotely controlled.

Electromagnetic: Relating to electric currents or fields and magnetic fields.

Emanate: To spread out from.

Evolve: Change gradually, especially from a simple to a more complex form.

Extraterrestrial: Originating from outside the earth.

Flux: Something that constantly changes.

Force field: An invisible barrier of protection or strength.

Frequency: The rate at which a vibration occurs in a wave (sound waves or electromagnetic waves), usually measured per second.

Galaxy: A system of millions or billions of stars, together with gas and dust, held together by gravity.

Gravity: A force that pulls two objects toward each other.

Halley's Comet: A comet that is visible from Earth every 76 years.

Hawking, Stephen: A 20-21st century cosmologist and theoretical physicist known for his work with black holes and relativity.

Hieroglyphics: Ancient symbols or writing.

Humanoid: A being that resembles a human.

Infrasound: Sound waves at a frequency below what humans can hear.

Intergalactic: Relating to two or more galaxies.

Kismet: Destiny or fate.

Milky Way: A large spiral galaxy made up of faint stars.

Multiverse: A group of universes, including; space, time, matter and energy.

Mutant: Change resulting from a genetic mutation.

Mutation: Is a mistake or a change in a living thing's DNA.

Nebula: Is an interstellar cloud of dust.

Quasar: The brightest objects in the universe, and produce huge amounts of energy.

Solar Plexus: Complex network of nerves (a plexus) located in the abdomen.

Stasis-field: Is a protected area of space in which time has been stopped – suspended animation.

Stratosphere: Is the second layer of the atmosphere as you go upward.

Subliminal: A hidden message, designed to be audible to the unconscious, or deeper mind.

Teleport: To be transported across space and distance instantly.

Telescope: An optical instrument to look at the stars, making them appear closer.

Theremin: Electronic musical instrument that is played without being touched.

Transistor: Works as an amplifier, it takes a tiny electric current at one end and produces a much bigger electric current at the other, as in a radio.

Transmission: The act of transferring something from one spot to another, like a radio or TV broadcast.

Ultrasonic: A frequency above the human ear's hearing limit of about 20,000 hertz.

Universe: The whole of space and all the stars, planets and forms of energy in it.

Uranus: The seventh planet in order from the sun.

Wormhole: Passage through space creating a shortcut through time and space.

ACKNOWLEDGEMENTS

I am grateful to the people who helped make this book a reality. First and foremost, my supportive and creative husband, Terry Coderre. He always had the solution to the plot holes. My editors, who found the plot holes: Isabelle Schumacher and Talya Pardo. My kids, who were very enthusiastic about this endeavor. I love you: Justin, Sophie and Kelly.

ABOUT THE AUTHOR

Ann Birdgenaw is a librarian in an elementary school and always wanted to write a book of her own. She was inspired to write this story by a strange beeping coming from a box in her garage. When COVID-19 hit Canada and everyone was in quarantine or lock down, she had lots of time to imagine being sucked through a wormhole to other planets and what wonderful things she might find there.

Ann lives in Montreal, Quebec, Canada with her family and two morkies: Bilbo and Sheba.

Visit Ann at https://www.goodreads.com/author/show/21269547.Ann_Birdgenaw

@abirdgenaw on Twitter

@annbirdbooks on Instagram

Stay Tuned for *Bilaluna*, Book 2 in the *Black Hole Radio* Series!

Hawk invites the new girl at school, Celeste, to visit the space club. They don't know it, but the Radio wants to give them a ride on the hyperspace highway....all the way to Pooponic's moon, Bilaluna, where the aliens need help to reverse the climate crisis that is killing their world. Join Hawk, Matt and Celeste on another intergalactic adventure as they are carried off by giant cyborg flies, race on the backs of cyborg roaches through an alien rainforest and sip nectar with the Queen Bee!

Be sure to look for the next book in the exciting series *Black Hole Radio!*

Printed in the USA
CPSIA information can be obtained
at www.ICGtesting.com
LVHW012142140524
780323LV00032B/898

9 781953 910486